This book belongs to

_____

THE UGLY
STEPSISTERS

WALT DISNEY FUN-TO-READ LIBRARY

TORONTO • NEW YORK • LONDON • SYDNEY • AUCKLAND

The Ugly Stepsisters   A Bantam Book/January 1986   All rights reserved.   Copyright © 1986 Walt Disney Productions.   This book may not be reproduced, in whole or in part, by mimeograph or any other means.

ISBN 0-553-05581-X

Published simultaneously in the United States and Canada.   Bantam Books are published by Bantam Books, Inc.   Its trademark, consisting of the words "Bantam Books" and the portrayal of a rooster, is Registered in U.S. Patent and Trademark Office and in other countries.   Marca Registrada.   Bantam Books, Inc., 666 Fifth Avenue, New York, New York 10103.   Printed in the United States of America   0 9 8 7 6 5 4 3 2 1

Today was the day Cinderella's stepsisters and stepmother were to arrive. Cinderella and Prince Charming waited at the entrance to their castle.

"There they are," said Cinderella. "Now
we must be sure to make this a happy visit.
After all, I have not seen my stepsisters and
stepmother for such a long time!"
"Yes, my love," said the Prince.

"Stepmother! Drizella and Anastasia! I am so happy to see you!" said Cinderella.

"My, Cinderella—how pretty you look," said the stepmother. "Would you send our clothes up right away? The girls must have their beauty rest. We've had a busy day."

"Yes, Stepmother—whatever you say," said Cinderella.

"Oh, boy! Look at all those boxes. It looks as if they are going to stay a long time," Jaq said to Gus. Then they hurried after Cinderella to see if they could help.

The sisters and their mother went up to rest. Then they came downstairs—just in time to eat. Cinderella had ordered the cook to make all the foods that the stepsisters loved.

"I hope you will be happy here," Cinderella told them.

"Of course we will be happy here," said the stepmother. "Why shouldn't we be happy?" she asked.

The Prince watched them and wondered. How could his kind, beautiful Cinderella have such mean and ugly stepsisters?

After supper, the sisters and their mother went to their rooms.

"Who does Cinderella think she is? She sure was showing off for us!" sneered Anastasia.

"Yes, and I don't think the Prince looked very happy—do you, Mother?" asked Drizella.

"Don't fuss so over Cinderella, my girls.
You are both more beautiful than she is,"
said their mother. "I just know the Prince was
wishing he had married one of you."

Meanwhile, Cinderella and her prince were taking a walk.

"I wonder how long they will stay," said the Prince. "They don't seem to be very happy, even here."

"If only they each had a husband as nice as you," said Cinderella. "Then they would be as happy as I am!

"I know! Let's surprise them and give
them a grand party!" said Cinderella.
"And we will ask all the fine men in the
kingdom to come to it!" said the Prince.
"Oh yes!" cried Cinderella.

The next morning Cinderella called her servants together. She told them about the party. "It is a surprise," she whispered. "Be sure not to let my stepsisters know. We'll say it's a party for some *very* important people."

But the stepsisters had been hiding at the bottom of the stairs. They heard the word *party*.

"What is all this about a party?" they wondered.

They heard Cinderella say it was a party for important people. The sisters ran to tell their mother.

"Important people, indeed!" said the sisters to their mother. "She just wants to show off again!"

"Don't worry, my dears," their mother
said. "Just listen to me. I have plans for
Cinderella's important party."

The sisters listened. Then they laughed.
"Oh, what fun!" they said.

In the library sat the Prince and
Cinderella. The Prince called out the name of
every man in the kingdom.

For each name, Cinderella wrote an invitation.

A servant carried all of the invitations into the hall.

That night, the sisters crept downstairs to the hall.

"We will take care of Cinderella and her party plans all right!" They laughed to each other. "Let's just put the invitations into the wrong envelopes. Then the guests will be very upset. They will not want to come to the party."

Jaq and Gus heard the stepsisters' evil plan. They waited until the sisters went back to bed.

"We don't have a minute to waste!"
cried Gus.

"We must put the invitations in order, or
Cinderella's party will be ruined," said Jaq.

Gus and Jaq worked all night. At last the
invitations were in order.

The next night, the stepsisters crept down to the kitchen.

"A little salt in the sugar . . ." said Anastasia.

"And a bit of soap in the flour . . ." added Drizella.

"Will make a lovely cake!" The sisters laughed to each other. Then they ran to tell their mother what they had done. They did not see Jaq and Gus.

"The food for the party will be ruined," cried Gus.

"There is only one thing to do," said Jaq. "We will have to pour out all the sugar and flour. Then the cook will have to buy more."

Jaq and Gus went to work.

The next morning, the cook was in for a big surprise. There was sugar and flour everywhere! She hurried to the store to get some more in time to bake the cake for Cinderella's party.

Meanwhile, Cinderella's servants were
making beautiful party dresses. The dresses
were to be part of the stepsisters' surprise.

But the sisters found out about the
dresses. They thought the dresses were for
Cinderella.

The stepsisters marched right into the
sewing room.

"These dresses are not good enough for Cinderella," they sneered. "Those ugly ribbons will have to come off!" And with that the sisters ripped up the dresses. Then they left the room.

"Now Cinderella won't have a single new dress to wear to her party!" they laughed.

Cinderella came into the sewing room to see how the dresses looked. But there were no new dresses. There were just tatters and rags. Her servants were crying. They told her what had happened.

"Oh, dear," said Cinderella. "I'm sure my stepsisters just wanted to help. Don't worry. I will help you finish the dresses in time."

"How kind she is," whispered the servants. "And how wicked those jealous stepsisters are."

At last it was the day of the ball.
While the servants were setting up the
ballroom, the stepsisters put their cat to work.
He ran through the ballroom and onto the
table. Plates and silverware flew through the air.

"Get that cat!" a servant shouted.
The servants chased the cat all around
the castle.

"Oh my, what a mess!" said Cinderella.
A servant tried to tell her about the cat.
"Well, well, don't worry. I will help you
clean up. We still have some time before the
party," Cinderella said.

Cinderella sang as she worked.
Soon everyone was happy and smiling.
Gus and Jaq helped too. At last the
ballroom sparkled and shone.

Meanwhile, the stepsisters were getting ready for the party.

"How embarrassed Cinderella will be! The guests will laugh at her when they see how her sisters dress for her parties!" they said.

"This will teach Cinderella to show off for my girls," said the stepmother.

At last it was time for the party. The
guests began to arrive.

"I hear that Cinderella has two stepsisters," said one duke.

"I wonder if they are as beautiful as Cinderella," said another.

Soon the hall was full of guests. The dukes and earls waited for Cinderella's stepsisters to come down.

The stepsisters and their mother walked to the top of the stairs.

"*Aagh!* Oh, no!" the guests gasped.
They cried out in horror because the
stepsisters were so ugly. All at once, the
men, young and old, ran for the door. They
hurried to get away.

"Oh, dear!" said Cinderella. "I invited all these nice people to meet you."

"But—who were the very important people you were giving the party for?" asked the stepmother.

"Why, <u>you</u> were," said Cinderella. "You and my stepsisters."

Just then the Prince whisked Cinderella onto the dance floor.

The ugly sisters began to cry.

"It serves them right. They are so mean and jealous," said Jaq to Gus. And they laughed as they danced the night away.